Sarah's Unicorn

Also by Bruce and Katherine Coville

THE FOOLISH GIANT

Sarah's Unicorn

Bruce and Katherine Coville

A Harper Trophy Book
Harper & Row, Publishers

Library of Congress Cataloging in Publication Data
Coville, Bruce.
    Sarah's unicorn.

    (A Lippincott I-like-to-read book)
    SUMMARY: Although she tries to keep her
friendship with Oakhorn a secret, Sarah's
wicked aunt finds out and is determined to rob
the unicorn of his magic.
    [1. Witches—Fiction. 2. Unicorns—
Fiction.] I. Coville, Katherine, joint author.
II. Title.
PZ7.C8344Sar   [E]   85-42749
ISBN 0-397-31872-3
ISBN 0-397-31873-1 (lib. bdg.)
ISBN 0-06-443084-7 (pbk.)

To Frank Halse, Jr.,
and
to forests everywhere

Once upon a time there was a little girl named Sarah.

She lived at the edge of a great forest.

That was nice.

Sarah lived with her Aunt Mag.
That was not so nice, because Mag
was a wicked witch.

Mag had been
a good witch
once.

Then a spell
blew up in her face.
It turned her
heart to stone.

That made Mag mean.

Soon the nice things about Mag
had changed.

Once she had told lovely fairy tales.

Now she told stories that kept
Sarah awake all night.

Once Mag had asked Sarah to
gather flowers.

Now she made her gather toads
and spiders.

Once Mag had been a good cook.
Now she made nothing but swamp
soup.

One night Mag ran out of toads.
"Sarah!" she yelled. "Go into the
forest. Get me a dozen toads."

Sarah didn't want to go. The forest was scary at night. But if she didn't go, Mag would make it rain in her bedroom for a week.

So she went.

The forest was dark.

Sarah shivered.

A branch snapped behind her.

Was something following her?

Sarah started to run.

She came to a clearing. In the center of the clearing stood an apple tree, covered with moonlight. It looked bright, and safe.

Sarah climbed the tree. She began
to feel better.

Then something stepped into the
clearing.

It was a unicorn.

Sarah knew about unicorns, of
course. But she had never seen one.

He was beautiful.

Sarah climbed down from the tree.

The unicorn didn't run.

She put out her hand.

He didn't run.

She scratched behind his ears.

"Ah!" said the unicorn. "That feels good."

Sarah jumped. "I didn't know unicorns could talk," she said.

"Pity," replied the unicorn. "You looked fairly clever. Keep scratching."

"My name is Sarah," said Sarah, as she scratched. "What's yours?"

"Oakhorn."

Sarah and Oakhorn became great friends. She began to sneak into the forest to see him.

They went for long rides together.

Sarah gave Oakhorn carrots.

And Oakhorn taught Sarah to talk
to the other animals.

Soon the night forest became a
friendly place for Sarah.

She played with the squirrels.

She tickled the bears.

And she told her best jokes to the rabbits.

She even made friends with a
ladybug. Her name was Mrs. Bunjy.

She made a nest in Sarah's pocket
and went everywhere with her.

Yet Sarah was still
sad sometimes, because
Mag was getting meaner
by the day.

One morning Sarah fell over Mag's
broom. She cut herself.

"That's what happens to clods like you," said Mag.

That made Mrs. Bunjy so mad she flew over to Mag and kicked her.

The witch didn't even feel it.

When Sarah showed the cut to
Oakhorn, he touched it with his horn.

The scab fell off.

The pain went away.

It had healed.

"How did you do that?" asked
Sarah.

"My horn has magic in it," said
Oakhorn.

When Mag saw that the cut had
healed, she knew Sarah had found
something magic.

But what?

She wanted to know. So she packed
her bag of tricks.

That night she followed Sarah into
the forest.

Sarah met Oakhorn at the apple tree.

Mag snorted with glee.

A unicorn! The magic in his horn could make her the greatest witch in the kingdom.

Sarah picked an apple.

Oakhorn bent his head to take it.

Mag jumped into the clearing.
Before Oakhorn could move she
had a rope around his neck.

"Take it off!" cried Sarah.

She grabbed Mag's arm.

Mag knocked Sarah down.

That made Mrs. Bunjy *really* angry.

She flew out of Sarah's pocket.

The other animals had heard
Sarah's cry. They began to gather at
the edge of the clearing . . . watching
. . . and waiting.

Mag tied Oakhorn to the apple
tree.

She took an ax from her bag.

It glittered in the moonlight.

"Now for that horn," she said.

Mrs. Bunjy landed on Mag's nose
and punched it.

That tickled.

Mag sneezed.

Mrs. Bunjy went flying—but so did
the ax.

The other animals rushed in. They knocked Mag down. The big bear sat on her. The little animals tickled her.

And Sarah untied Oakhorn.

There was fire in his eye.

"Bring the witch here," he said.

The bears stood Mag in front of
him. He pointed his horn at her.

"No!" cried Mag. "Don't hurt me!"

Oakhorn snorted.

"Wait, Oakhorn," said Sarah. "She used to be nice. Can't you fix her? Please?"

Oakhorn looked disgusted.

But he touched Mag softly with his horn.

She turned pale. She put her hand
on her heart.

Then she began to smile. "You
broke the spell!" she said.

She gave Oakhorn
a kiss. He made an
awful face.

Everyone was happy.

Except Mrs. Bunjy. She had a
headache. So Oakhorn fixed that too.
Later, Mag and Sarah made her a
little house.

Then they all got along just fine.

And sometimes at night, when the
moon was high, Oakhorn would
come to Sarah's window.

He would take her on his back . . .

. . . and they would ride till dawn,
dancing on the moonbeams.

Unicorns can do that, you know.